It Was Meant To Be

$\mathcal{I}$T WAS MEANT TO BE

Christina Heseltine

AuthorHouse™
1663 Liberty Drive
Bloomington, IN 47403
www.authorhouse.com
Phone: 1-800-839-8640

© 2012 by Christina Heseltine. All rights reserved.

No part of this book may be reproduced, stored in a retrieval system, or transmitted by any means without the written permission of the author.

Published by AuthorHouse   10/02/2012

ISBN: 978-1-4772-3463-1 (sc)
ISBN: 978-1-4772-3464-8 (e)

Any people depicted in stock imagery provided by Thinkstock are models, and such images are being used for illustrative purposes only.
Certain stock imagery © Thinkstock.

This book is printed on acid-free paper.

Because of the dynamic nature of the Internet, any web addresses or links contained in this book may have changed since publication and may no longer be valid. The views expressed in this work are solely those of the author and do not necessarily reflect the views of the publisher, and the publisher hereby disclaims any responsibility for them.

Chapter 1

It was a man's room. The large open log fire, deep, comfortable leather chairs; the fully stocked drinks cabinet, and a somewhat organised scattering of magazines on a low table. Three of the walls were covered floor to the high ceiling with books.

'Where are you Dad?' the muffled call could be heard through the thick door. 'I'm here Davey, in the library. Tom was at the top of the rail ladder that ran around the walls. He heard the door open 'Dad, I'd like you to meet Heather Thornton'. Tom smiled 'so this is one of the special young ladies you've been telling me about'. Heather called out 'I've been anxious to meet you for a long time Mr Dunbar'. The smile froze on Tom's face, his spine stiffened as he turned and looked down. He stared, opened his mouth but there was no sound. The world was spinning around, his hands slipped and he fell from the ladder.

Davey held Heather in his arms. 'Dads unconscious but appears there are no broken bones, Doc says he should come round shortly and be OK in a couple of days'. He squeezed her arm, I know the sight of you makes me weak at the knees but I didn't think you would have the same affect on my Dad. They laughed. 'We'll stay with him for a while, just hope he has happy dreams'. Tom was in another world, seemingly reliving his entire life.

Chapter 2

(many years in the past)

Dampness hung in the air following the morning's heavy rainfall. Persistent dark clouds did little to brighten up the grey buildings. Tom shivered, pulling his thin jacket tighter. It was already too small for him, even without the books tucked inside close to his chest. The brightly lit library was welcoming as he entered the warm interior, this for Tom was a wonderland of both fictional escapism and total reality.

Mrs Main smiled as she watched him approach and put the three books on the counter. 'You got through these in a hurry Tommy, they're not due back for another two weeks'.

Tom merely grinned at her, accepted his 'reader's tickets', and headed for the myriad aisles of precious books. At a snail's pace he went from one group to another letting his fingers trail along the bookends. His vivid imagination gave him a feeling of excitement just reading the titles.

Mrs Main left the books she was sorting and turned as Tom put his selections on the counter. 'H.G. Wells again Tommy, this must be the third time you've been Around the World. You planning to be the next Phileas Fogg then'?

'Well it won't be in a balloon, Mrs Main, but when I get to all those places I'll send you postcards'.

She laughed, 'Well let's see, you're 12 now and I retire in 3 years time so you'll have to get your skates on. Here, I've got a plastic carrier bag you can put the books in, it might rain again before you get home. Enjoy your dreams, love'.

Tom heard the chime of the church clock and started to run. "Be sure you're home before Dad" his Mother had warned. Tom raced up the stairs to the flat on the fourth floor of the tenement building. Already he could hear the gruff angry voice through the unopened door. 'Where the hell is he. Can't even tell the bloody time yet, little bugger should've been here hours ago. I've a damned good mind to make him go without his supper'.

Tom entered the kitchen as Alice was putting the plates on the table. 'Sorry, Mum, I forgot to look at the clock in the library, I didn't think it was so late'. Billy Murray glared at his son. 'Library, he grunted, that's the trouble with you boy, always got your nose stuck in a book. Would be a damned sight better if you were out on the football field like any normal lad your age. A weak, bloody sissy, that's you' he shouted, waving his knife menacingly.

Alice looked sympathetically at Tom but knew it would be better not to say anything. They ate their meal in silence. After a short time Billy pushed his empty plate away, washed his hands and face at the kitchen sink, then putting on his jacket and cloth cap he left the flat without saying a word. There was really no need for him to say he was off to the pub, Tom and Alice knew the routine well, in fact it was a relief to both of them when he did go out.

'I was cleaning Mrs Jacob's house today and she was telling me about her son Ralph going to boarding school next week.

She was packing a trunk with his new school clothes and she told me to get rid of the rest of his things to any of the charity shops. I kept out a jacket and trousers which I can alter to fit you, come and try them on'. Tom hated the idea but had become accustomed over the years to wearing second hand clothes. He put the jacket on, it was on the large side but with the sleeves shortened it would look alright. Anyway, he thought, it would be a big improvement on what he was wearing now, this one even had a silk lining. The trousers would need taking in at the waist and hips. Alice was clever in making alterations and no one would ever guess, he hoped. 'Mrs Jacobs also told me to clear out some of his old books and I thought you might like to have them'. Tom's eyes lit up when Alice brought out the bag. There was a typical selection of boy's adventure stories and travel books with pictures of the world's capital cities. Tom hugged his mother and took himself off to his bed in the corner of the kitchen.

Some time later they heard Billy singing loudly as he climbed the stairs, both hoping it meant he was in a good mood. He was fumbling with the keys trying to unlock the door and Alice told Tom to go and open the door. On entering the flat Billy staggered to the kitchen table. He swayed as he struggled to get the half bottle of whisky and the bottle of beer out of his jacket pocket. 'Get me a glass' he demanded in a slurred voice. Alice put a tumbler on the table in front of him then moved back to the chair by the fire and took up her knitting again. Billy slurped as he drank beer from the bottle, some of it dribbling down his shirt. 'Wally Smart's boy is trying out for the junior team on Saturday, and look what I've got' he sneered, looking at Tom who had returned to his bed and was propped up reading. 'A good for nothing bookworm is what I've got—no, never mind the book, just a worm'. He rose suddenly and lurched to where Tom was lying, the books Alice had brought home were spread across the bed. Billy scooped them up, turned and threw them into the open fire. Alice uttered a cry and made an effort to retrieve the books. Billy twisted her arm and pushed her against the wall. A scream rose in Tom's throat and he rushed at his father, fists flying, feet kicking out. Billy Murray was a fairly tall, heavily built man with powerful arms. He grabbed Tom by the throat holding him at arms length. Alice tried to get between them to shield her son. 'he's only a boy, Billy, let him go' she pleaded. 'You mamby, pamby little shit, well there'll be snowballs in hell boy before you charge at me again', and Billy laughed cruelly as he slapped Tom several times across the face and let him drop to the floor. Billy shuffled past the table, picking up the whisky bottle as he went through to the bedroom.

Tom was limp, barely conscious. Alice helped him back to bed and brought a damp cloth to bathe his face. 'I hate him

Mum, really hate him, I wish he was dead. Why don't we leave him Mum, we don't need him'. 'Hush Tommy, you know running away never solved anything. Sometimes your Dad doesn't know his own strength and the drink just turns him into a mad man'. There was a resigned look on her face. 'Maybe if you tried to take an interest in football or other sports Tommy you would get on a lot better with him and maybe we might have a little peace around here'.

Tom did make an effort to get into the football team and competed in athletic events. He had a natural ability and could have succeeded but it was obvious to the team coaches he didn't really enjoy sports and wouldn't make the effort they needed. It was no surprise that he was never selected to play for any of the school teams. Being a consistent winner of various scholastic prizes made no impression on his father, and over the years they grew further apart.

Chapter 3

It was the end of term presentation of certificates and prizes. Alice sat in the third row, flushed with pride each time Tom's name was called out as the first prize winner in most subjects, but no sporting trophies. Billy had refused to attend the ceremony. Tom and Alice looked at the cheerful face of the Head Master who was sitting across from them. 'Tom has been our star pupil this term, you should be very proud of him Mrs Murray. With his ability he should be encouraged to pursue further education, there's no doubt in my mind Tom would secure a place at University quite easily'. Alice gazed out the window as Mr Shields continued speaking. 'Tom has told me there are financial problems at home, but he would be eligible for grants to assist towards tuition fees and buying books. If you could see your way to letting him pursue this opportunity, Mrs Murray, I am positive it will lead to a very bright future for him'. 'Tom's right about the money problems, Mr Shields, and there are some other problems. It's something I must talk over with his father' she said quietly. They left the school with Alice taking Tom's arm, looking up into his face, she was feeling immensely proud. He had grown to almost 6 feet and though still on the thin side she knew he would fill out in time. He was going to be a bigger man than his father.

'What do you think he'll say, Mum'? Alice hesitated, 'I'm not sure, Tommy, you know he has mellowed a bit over the years and that ulcer has made him cut down on the drink. He's not fighting and throwing his weight around as he did before. Maybe if we handle it right he might see it our way'. She was hoping fervently that Billy would agree.

The evening meal was its usual ritual. Alice had taken care to prepare Billy's favourite food and special dessert. Billy ate in silence, the evening newspaper propped up in front of him. As Alice poured tea into the cups she tried to adopt a light conversational tone, 'Billy, Tommy's headmaster spoke to me at the prize giving today, he says Tommy did very well in the exams and he should take the chance to go to University'. There was a sound like a muffled growl from

It Was Meant To Be

Billy. And where's the money to come from for that little lark, eh'? 'Well, Mr Shields said Tommy would qualify for a grant and he would be staying at home so that's no problem'. 'No problem! So that's it then. We've to work ourselves into an early grave just so he can skive off sticking his head in books and learning other arty-farty crafts. Well take it from me Lady there *is* a bloody problem, Billy shouted, the answer is NO. It's time he was made to realise what life is all about, start growing up, earn some money to keep himself and put something in to run this place he snarled. So, we've kept him bloody long enough, he can look after himself for a change'. Standing up, he glared at Alice, his fists clenched. 'For too damned long I've let you get away with giving him these big ideas, "Tommy needs a place to study", so we had to move to a bigger house, "Tommy needs this, Tommy needs that", always letting him think he was better than the rest of us. Well that's all over. He's coming to the yard with me on Monday. I spoke to the gaffer and he'll take him on as a helper. If he's any good he might get the chance to learn a trade'.

Tom ran from the flat and for hours he walked the dark streets. Anger and frustration boiled inside of him, the hatred for his father was intense. Old swine, he thought, he's not going to get me into that stinking yard. I'll take off first, get as far away from this god-forsaken place as soon as possible. There's nothing for me here. I'll go to New

Zealand or Canada, they're always advertising for young people. I can make it on my own. Then as he trudged home he thought of his mother, she would be left to bear the brunt of his father's anger and possible physical violence. Tom's shoulders slumped, no, he couldn't do that to her, he loved her too much to do that, she needed his protection now. But he vowed Billy wouldn't have the last word, he would shape his own future.

Chapter 4

Tom started work in the yard, it was boring and mundane but he got along well with the men in the squad. At times they would tease him, Imagine Billy the madman Murray's boy not knowing anything about football, boxing and drinking they laughed. While they would sit around during meal breaks discussing the weekend sport, Tom would be by himself studying, he had enrolled in a class at night school for a course in technical drawing and architecture. The men gave him nicknames like "the brain-box kid" but all in good humour.

Tom worked with the fabricators and daily went to the office for drawings of the plates they were working on. He would look enviously at draughtsmen sitting on their high stools working on the slanted boards in front of them and thought wistfully of what it would be like to have such a job. On one occasion he went into the staff offices and on their notice board he saw an internal vacancy ad for Trainee Draughtsmen. The closing date for applications was the following day, he stood for some minutes then straightened his shoulders and approached the Senior Draughtsman, George Stevens, asking if he could apply for the job. George looked at the lad in the grubby boiler suit and hobnail boots. 'I've been taking the technical drawing course at night school and in addition to what I was taught at school I have a good basic understanding of what is needed.' George was impressed with the language he used. He noted the strong jawline and the steely determination in the boy's eyes. 'We normally take lads direct from school, Tom, but the PR people have been making noises about "promoting from within", which was the reason for putting the notice on the board. I'd like to see how you draw', and he went to a board in the corner of his office. 'Look at this, it's a small section which you can copy but try adjusting it to the new scale figures at the bottom'. Tom was nervous as George looked over his shoulder while he worked on the drawing but in a short while he felt an easy familiarity in making the necessary changes. 'That looks not bad Tom. On the surface I don't see why we shouldn't try to get you on the scheme. I'll have a word with Mr McLean, if you're really interested'. Tom at first only nodded his head then finally managed to get the words out, 'Mr Stevens that would be terrific, I would work hard and and ... Now hold on Tom, I said I'd *talk* to Mr McLean, it is entirely up to him so don't get your hopes up too high. Here, fill out this application form and we'll take it from there'.

Tom was in a fever of excitement. Each time he went into the drawing office he would glance towards George Stevens' office, sometimes their eyes met and he would get a nod in response to his smile. Two weeks passed and Tom's hopes were fading. On Wednesday of the following week, as Tom picked up the drawings for the East Yard, he heard someone calling his name and turned to see George beckoning him. 'Mr McLean was impressed with your school exam results Tom, as a matter of fact he called your old headmaster, Mr Shields, and he gave you a very good recommendation. I've been told that we can take you on in the drawing office as a trainee. You will be on the college day-release scheme which means you can cancel night school'.

Alice was overjoyed at her son's news. 'You'll have to get some new clothes, Tom. I've been saving up for a new coat but you need it more than me'. Tom laughed, 'Now wait a minute Mum, have you forgotten, I've got money of my own now, I can take care of myself. Any technical gear I need I can get through the yard at a discount price and repay them so much a week over a period of time'.

Billy Murray made no comment. He had long since given up trying to find some ground of common interest with his son. That night, after a bout of heavy drinking, he was sitting at the kitchen table muttering, 'don't suppose you could handle a welding torch or a drill like any normal man eh, no it has to be pencils and paper for you, haven't even got a girlfriend eh, don't suppose you know how to handle a woman eh, maybe you prefer men, eh, that would be just like you' he sneered. Tom refused to rise to the bait, he went through to his own room to listen to music and read. Let the old swine rant and rave by himself.

Chapter 5

Jim, and other trainee draughtsmen, were coming out of the main door of the College. 'We're going to the coffee house across the street, Tom, fancy Joining us'.

The six of them were seated at a corner booth. 'Hey look over there, two good looking birds' said Harry and all eyes turned to look, 'The dark haired one is Joanne Martin, I wouldn't mind a date with her' he continued, 'heard she's taking an arts course, maybe I should change courses' he laughed. 'I hear her old man never let's her out of his sight 'Kevin said 'old-fashioned ideas, only somebody from the top drawer is good enough for his daughter. Guess that means none of us are in with a chance'.

Tom thought he had never seen a more beautiful girl. Her long chestnut coloured hair fell in waves down her back, even from a distance he could see her eyes were a deep hazel colour, the small nose twitched as she laughed at something her friend was saying. She turned looking directly into Tom's eyes. Blushing she quickly looked away. 'I think I'll go over and ask her for a date' said Tom. Jim laughed,' bet you a pint of best bitter she gives you the brush off'. You're on' said Tom rising from the table. Heads turned as the handsome young man worked his way between tables and crossed the floor. Tom had reached his maximum height of six feet one, his thick brown hair crowned a high forehead, wide spaced brown eyes and a straight nose over a sensitive mouth.

When he stopped at their table the two girls looked up. Joanne lowered her eyes while Beth smiled up at Tom. 'Would you girls mind if I sit at your table, can I get you another coffee or something else'?. Joanne looked flustered, she picked up her books from the chair without looking at Tom. 'It's getting late Beth, we should be leaving now'. Beth raised her eyebrows and shrugged her shoulders, 'thanks anyway, maybe another time'.

It Was Meant To Be

Tom watched as they left the shop and rejoined Jim and the others. 'You owe me one' said Jim, 'I could have told you no one has ever gotten even close to getting a date with Miss Joanne Martin. Not even your good looks could melt that iceberg Tom. But little Beth looked quite taken, you'd do better to you set your cap in that direction'. Tom couldn't get Joanne out of his mind. When he closed his eyes he could see her shining hair, bright eyes and the blush on her cheeks, he had to get to know her better.

At college the following week he waited outside the building and watched as Joanne and Beth ran down the stairs. He crossed in front of them. 'Hi girls, how about letting me buy you that coffee now'. Simultaneously Beth said yes please, Joanne said no thank you. 'Oh come on Joanne, we always go for a coffee anyway' . . . 'No, Beth, Joanne said in a quiet firm voice. I think we should go straight home'. 'Well you can go if you want to but I'm willing to accept the gentleman's kind offer' said Beth smiling coquettishly at Tom. Tom watched Joanne walk away, he had no alternative but to take Beth to the coffee shop. Beth was a petite attractive girl with short blond hair, blue/green eyes, pouted lips under a small straight nose. She was talking very quickly, asking questions seemingly without waiting for answers. Tom was very quiet, looking out of the window in the direction that Joanne had gone. There was a moment's silence. 'You really wanted to be here with Joanne, didn't you?' The question cut across Tom's thoughts and he looked directly at Beth. 'I'm sorry Beth. I didn't mean to be so obvious but you're right, I did want to meet Joanne, perhaps get to know her better. You're her friend, can you tell me about her'. Beth sighed, a wan smile on her lips. 'Well I don't know a great deal, we only meet in College and get together for a coffee afterwards. She has told me she is an only child, apparently her mother died when Joanne was born. Her father seems to be rather old fashioned, very possessive. She's not allowed to go dancing or date anyone. Our coming to the coffee house after college is about the only social time she has. There really isn't much more I can tell you, Tom'.

Joanne opened the front door, walked across the large lobby and started up the stairs. 'Is that you, Joanne, you're home earlier than usual, everything alright?'

She turned, going downstairs into her father's office. 'I didn't go for a coffee with Beth today that's why I'm early.' 'Just as well' he sniffed, 'I'm not certain from what you tell me of her family that she is the best companion for you. Come and listen to the speech I'm preparing for the Board of St. Margarets. I won't accept the Chairmanship nomination again, just keep my seat on the Board. I am seriously considering the offer of that Consultancy position in South Africa.'

Two weeks previously she hadn't given much thought to moving to South Africa, not that she would have had any choice. Her father made all the decisions and would have brooked no argument. Now that she had seen Tom Murray and heard him speak she was suddenly confused. Just to see him had aroused feelings in her which she didn't know existed. His voice broke into her thoughts. 'You're not paying attention, Joanne. Do you have a comment about my hospital Board speech.' 'Would it make any difference if I did?' He looked up at her sharply. Did I really say those words, she asked herself. She felt herself shake, she had never in her life spoken to him like that. 'I'm sure you must have studying to do,' he said in a stern manner, 'I shall see you for dinner at 7 o'clock.'

She could feel the heat rise in her neck and knew her face was red. In her room she sat for a long time studying her reflection in the dressing table mirror. She had never critically looked at herself, never questioned whether she might be considered plain or pretty, it had never mattered before. In the mirror she could also see Tom's handsome face, she fantasized over what it would be like to be with him. She agonised over her refusal to accept his offer of coffee and wondered if he would ask her again. If he ever asks me again, I'll definitely accept, she thought.

Chapter 6

On reaching home Tom found his father slumped across the table, obviously in a drunken stupor. 'Is that you, Tommy?' His mother called from the bedroom. Tom went to the bedroom door, 'Yes, is everything alright? I see Dad's in his usual euphoric state,' he said sarcastically. At that point there was a noise behind him and Tom turned to see his father rise from the table and lurch towards the bedroom door. 'What you doin' there?' he shouted at Tom. 'Get away from that door you good-for-nothin' . . . he tripped, falling heavily against the wall. Tom put out a hand and caught him before he dropped to the floor. 'Take your hands off me, you're not so big that I can't still wallop the shit out of you' and he swung wildly at Tom's head. Alice came out of the bedroom, 'Stop this madness' she cried. Tom turned and saw the swelling on her forehead and the blackened eye. Something snapped in Tom's head, he seemed to be looking at the scene from the outside. He saw himself pick his father up by the lapels of his jacket and start to punch him about the face, the chest and stomach in a cold fury. Every punch carried years of hate and frustration and were delivered with such a cold, murderous, rage that even he was afraid of what was happening. 'You're killing him, Tommy, you're killing him. Stop, you don't understand, it's not what you're thinking.' His mother's voice finally penetrated and he let the blood covered body slump to the floor. 'I'm sorry, Mum, I can't take any more of this man. Look what he's done to you, I won't stand by and . . .' 'I'll explain in a minute Tommy. Help me clean him up and get him to bed. You shouldn't have hit him like that, Tommy, you might have killed him.' Best thing that could have happened, thought Tom. Billy was asleep breathing heavily. Alice had seen him with worse injuries from his many fights over the years, he would recover.

They were seated at the kitchen table. 'Tommy, I know what you're thinking, but your dad didn't hit me. I had a dizzy spell going down the stairs today, it's been happening a lot these last few months. I fell hitting my head on the bottom step. I was unconscious for a bit. The Doctor's been out, he wants me to go to the hospital tomorrow for a check up.' 'I'm sorry Mum, but when I saw your face I just lost all reason. When you think of all that's happened in the past, I just thought he had taken his bad temper out on you again.' He reached over and took her hand. 'You should've gone straight to the hospital, Mum, you might have concussion, it could be serious.' Alice looked at him, pain and weariness etched on her face. She suddenly looked so much older. 'I'm tired now, Tommy. I think a good night's sleep would help us both.'

Billy was a sorry looking sight the next morning and had little recollection of what had happened. 'Did I come home like this, Alice?' he asked. 'You had a bit of a fall, Billy, I don't think there is any lasting damage.' There were tears in his eyes, 'I'm sorry, Alice, those marks on your face, did I hit you lass?' Alice shook her head and explained what had happened, 'I have an appointment at the hospital at 2 o'clock.' 'I'll go with you, I can . . .' 'No,' Tom interrupted, 'I'm taking Mum to hospital.'

Billy closed his lips tightly, the days of arguing with his son were over. If he were to admit the truth, he was now a little afraid of Tom.

Tom was explaining to the Consultant that his father was unwell and could not come to the hospital at this time, he didn't feel the need to tell him that Billy was most likely in a drunken stupor at home. 'The news is not good, Mr Murray. I'll be perfectly frank with you, the tests indicate that your mother has a brain tumour and it is inoperable.' Tom could hardly breathe, 'Are you saying my mother is dying, Doctor?' 'I'm sorry, Mr Murray, but it is only a matter of time.' 'How much time?'. 'Again, I'm sorry, we can't be certain, really it could be months, weeks, anytime. I assure you we will do everything possible to lessen her suffering.' Anytime, anytime, it was the only word Tom heard as he drove home. God it couldn't be true, not his mother, not this strong woman whose love had protected him all these years. Now when he had the chance to make life a bit more pleasant for her this should happen, was there any justice in this world.

He entered the flat and found his father as he had left him, only a little more drunk and a little more dead to the world. Tom looked at him and experienced mixed feelings of loathing and yet pity. Billy Murray, the hard man, the man nothing could touch. But Tom recognised the weak, vulnerable side. This man whose very existence revolved around his wife, but who would never admit to it. How would he cope now. 'You'd better get yourself straightened up, Mum's very sick and you're not going to the hospital in a drunken state to cause her any more pain.' Billy looked at his son and prepared to lash out, but the look in Tom's eyes and the square set of his jaw dissuaded Billy from such action.

The Sister was standing at the entrance to the ward and motioned to them as they approached. 'Please wait just a moment, Mr Murray, the doctor is with your wife, he should be out very soon.' They sat on the hard bench, each of them locked in their own thoughts. The Consultant approached and spoke to Tom, 'Your Mother . . .' 'Just a minute,' interrupted Billy, 'It's my wife your talking about, if you've anything to say, say it to me.' Tom looked at the Consultant and raised his eyebrows a fraction. 'Mr Murray, I regret there has been a serious deterioration in your wife's condition, I don't think . . .' Billy lunged through the door to the ward 'Alice, Alice,' he shouted running down the length of the ward towards a bed shrouded in curtains. Tom found him lying across the still body in the bed, 'I'm sorry Alice, I'm sorry. I'll make it up to you, honest, honest,' he cried, tears running down his cheeks, falling on the cool white sheet. Tom looked at the shrivelled up man, the once hardened individual who never showed any love, fear or emotion of any kind, now crumbling before him. Alice opened her eyes, she stroked Billy's head. 'I know what you mean, Billy, I know. Be good to our Tommy.' The effort of saying even these few words seemed to drain her of all energy. She looked up once at Tom and smiled, then slipped into a coma. Tom and Billy were with Alice when she died at 3:30 the following morning.

There weren't many people at the funeral. Neither Billy or Alice had any brothers or sisters still alive, the only relatives were distant cousins. Alice had asked to be cremated, no fuss no bother, was the way she had put it.

Chapter 7

Billy watched Tom as he packed two suitcases. 'You don't have to move out you know, you've got your own room and things, what else do you need?' he said gruffly. Tom looked at him. The grey unshaven face, the clothes seeming to hang on the shrunken body. Tom could feel pity for him but there was no love, nothing that would make him stay any longer. He had watched him drinking steadily since his mother had died three months previously. There was a strike of manual workers at the yard and this meant he hardly ever left the flat. 'I'm 22 now, it's time I set up on my own. I've got my own friends and just want to lead my own life. And you'd do yourself a favour by laying off the booze, you're just killing yourself.' Billy clenched his fists, 'Who the hell are you to tell me what to do' he snarled, 'I'll god-damned do what I like without a little shit like you poking his nose in. Go on, get out then, who the hell needs you anyway, eh?'

Tom picked up the suitcases and walked out of the door without a backward glance, he didn't see the tears in his father's eyes or the trembling lips forming the unspoken name, Tommy.

Chapter 8

Several months had passed and Joanne and Beth had become part of the regular group meeting in the coffee house. The mutual attraction between Tom and Joanne was obvious and at times they seemed to be oblivious of the others at the table. It became routine for the group to drift away, leaving them on their own. 'But surely if I met your father, Joanne, I could convince him of how much we feel for each other. It's stupid in this day and age we should have to meet like this. I want to take you to the theatre, out for dinner, go dancing. The normal things couples do.'

'Give me just a bit longer, Tom.' There was a worried frown on her forehead, 'You remember I told you about my father being offered the Consultancy position in South Africa, I believe he has decided to accept it. He just takes it for granted that I will go with him, it would never enter his head that I might want to stay here, I'm still a child to him.' 'South Africa', he exclaimed 'that's half way round the world, Joanne.' He held her hand. 'We love each other Joanne. I'm not going to give you the old cliche of "made in heaven" stuff, but I just know we were meant for each other. The days of "must do what daddy says" are long gone. You are old enough to make your own decisions.' 'I need more time. Be patient just a little longer Tom.' A few days later Tom watched Joanne as she came down the steps of the college, his ready smile fading at the expression on her face. 'Let's skip the coffee today and just go for a walk, Tom.' They walked in the nearby park and sat on the bench by the pond. 'I spoke to my father last night' she began, 'I have never seen him so furious. He accused me of sneaking behind his back, seeing men without his knowledge. Tom, it was awful.' Tom sat quietly holding her hand. 'It's the first real argument we have ever had, probably because I never had the courage to disagree with him before. I told him I had met someone I liked very much, someone I wanted to be with. He ranted on about how much I owed him, how I wasn't old enough to know anything about men. Finally he refused to let me invite you home and forbade me to see you again. It was like a scene from one of those period 18th century dramas. He went on about South Africa, spoke as though there was nothing else to discuss and it was only weeks away. He scared me.'

Tom felt the pain of helplessness then fury and anger as he watched Joanne shed the silent tears. 'He can't keep us apart, Joanne. We're going to be together for the rest of lives, this was meant to be'.

They walked on and seemingly without either of them having to put it into words, for the first time they climbed the stairs to Tom's flat. Tom opened the bottle and poured the deep red wine into two glasses. They touched glasses, took a sip of wine and kissed lightly at first and then passionately. Holding each other tightly they sank to the carpet. 'Joanne, I . . .'. She smiled, gently pulled his head down until their open lips met, tongues touching, erotic senses heightened, finally coming together and experiencing the ecstasy of mutual love.

A month later they were celebrating Tom's college graduation and hung the framed degree certificate on the wall. 'This is our passport to the future, Joanne. How does it feel to be marrying an up and coming architect.' 'Sounds good to me, you can design and build our dream house somewhere.' 'I'm still keen on going to Canada, Joanne, it's a young country with lot's of opportunities. I think we should start making plans, don't you?' I like the sound of Canada too and, well, things might be moving in the right direction. Dad's accepted your invitation to dinner on Friday. He's been so very quiet recently I don't quite know what to expect. I Guess we should just be thankful he's dropped the "forbidding this and that" nonsense. Maybe he is finally accepting the inevitable.'

Tom enjoyed cooking. His mothers recipe books were used frequently and with some of his own innovations he had concocted some quite exotic meals. But tonight had to be very special. He planned everything very carefully deciding to keep it simple. Joanne had given him some idea of her father's tastes and he had put together a menu of; clear chicken soup, sole meuniere with asparagus tips and parsley potatoes followed by a variety of cheeses with oatmeal and wafer biscuits. The two bottles of expensive wine were cooling in the fridge. Everything looked perfect. The table set, candles ready to be lit, soft instrumental music on the turntable. Nothing must go wrong. Joanne and her father arrived punctually at 7:30. Tom started to kiss Joanne but drew back when he saw the expression in her fathers eyes. He poured the drinks and suffered agonies over the slightly stilted conversation. The soup was delicious and the fish was done to perfection. The atmosphere was becoming decidedly lighter, much to Tom and Joanne's relief. Tom was in the kitchen getting the cheese board and biscuits when there was a loud banging on the door. 'I'll get it' Joanne called out and he heard her open the door. Tom froze when he heard the loud, slurred, drunken voice; 'Who are you, where's Tommy?'

Tom came into the room just as Billy tripped on the carpet. He fell forward pulling the table cloth and scattered everything onto the floor. He lay on the floor crying like a child. 'This is the day she died, my Alice, this is the day she died.' Shock and fear were etched on Joanne's face as she looked at the man lying on the floor, 'Who is this man Tom?' 'He's my father' replied Tom in a voice drained of emotion. Frank Martin looked around with disdain and loathing. 'Get your coat Joanne, it's time we left for home' he said coldly. Joanne looked tearfully and silently at Tom, appealing to him to say something. Tom was unable to speak, he could only think of his future happiness destroyed by the miserable low life lying on his carpet.

Chapter 9

They met a few nights later. They were walking, Tom chuckled 'lets splash out, we'll get some fish and chips at Angios and have a few drinks in the apartment'. They were sitting close together on the couch, 'I don't know what to do Tom, he refuses to let me talk about you. All I get is stupid statements about associating with trash.' 'I've never told you much about my family, Joanne, or the type of life I had. My mother was a wonderful person, I loved her very dearly. My father, he shrugged, well you saw for yourself. He's been like this all his life. I thought I had put it all behind me but I guess you can't ever really escape your past.' He sighed deeply, defeat showing in his eyes. 'Your father could be right Joanne, maybe

I'm not the person for you. All I know for certain is that no one could love you more than I do'. Joanne's expression was a mixture of smiles and tears. 'And the one thing I am most certain of is that I couldn't find a better father for our baby.'

Tom stared at her, his expressions changing from disbelief, wonder, excitement and tender love. He took her in his arms holding her gently, her head resting on his shoulder, he stroked her long silken hair. 'This could be the answer we've been looking for Joanne. There's no way your father could object to our being together now. We must marry as soon as possible. We've got to confront him now, we have a lot of plans to make and the sooner the better.'

'Tom, let me talk to him first, tonight. Hopefully he will see sense, if not then I'm prepared to come here for good.' 'Ok, but you must call me tomorrow for sure.' He held her face in his large hands. 'Remember Joanne, regardless of what he says we're going to be married as soon as possible. It might not be the way we planned it, but this baby is going to be the first of many, we both want a big family don't we?' 'Well I think six would be about enough but let's get this little one produced first' she smiled.

Tom stared at the phone willing it to ring. He had no appetite. Mixing a whisky and water he sat trying to read the

It Was Meant To Be

paper but the words were a jumble. By 6 o'clock he could wait no longer. He dialled the number and on the third ring it was answered by Frank Martin. Tom cleared his throat. 'Hello Doctor Martin it's Tom, I would like to speak to Joanne please.' The voice was cold. 'Joanne can't come to the phone, she is unwell.' 'She was perfectly alright yesterday, what's happened, can I come over to see her?' 'It would not be convenient for you to visit, no doubt Joanne will be in touch. Now if you will excuse me.' The line was dead. Tom paced the floor like a caged tiger. He tried to imagine what might have happened when Joanne told her father about the baby, what had he said to make her suddenly ill or was that just his story. The following day Tom telephoned several times, there was no reply. By the time he was ready to leave the office he had made up his mind. He drove to Joanne's house, rang the bell and waited. Several times he rang but there was no response. He was starting down the steps when an older woman approached. 'Can I help you,' she asked. 'I was calling for Joanne but there doesn't appear to be anyone at home.' 'Well that's right no one is here at the moment. Miss Joanne is in the nursing home, Doctor Martin is with her.' Tom stared at the woman with a vacant, uncomprehending look on his face. 'Nursing home, which nursing home?' 'It's the private clinic, St. Margaret's in the Park. I don't think they allow visitors.' her voice trailed off as Tom ran towards his car.

The young girl at reception looked up, smiling a little nervously, apparently new at the Job. 'I'm Joanne Martin's fiancee' Tom began, 'Can you tell me her room number please?' She looked down at some sheets on the desk. 'Miss Martin's been through her operation and . . .' Just then an older woman came out of the inner office. 'I'll handle this matter, Jean, why don't you take care of the filing.' The girl blushed, with her eyes down she hurried into the office. 'How can I help you Mr mm?' 'Murray, Tom Murray. I am Joanne Martin's fiancee. I've just learned she was admitted here last night. I've been unable to contact Dr Martin, and I would like to see Joanne.' 'I'm afraid that's not possible, she is in recovery and the only visitors permitted are her immediate family.' 'But I'm her fiancee.' 'I'm sorry, Mr Murray, my instructions are that the only visitor allowed is her father.' 'The young girl who was just here, she spoke of an operation, what is that all about?'

'I'm sorry, I'm not at liberty to discuss the matter. I suggest you speak directly to Dr Martin.' 'I was told he was here.' Her face was expressionless. 'I can't confirm that Mr Murray, again I can only suggest you get in touch with Dr Martin at home.' As Tom left the building the woman pressed a buzzer. 'The young man has left Dr Martin.'

Chapter 10

Tom phoned the following morning. A pleasant voice announced 'Dr Martin's residence, how can I help.' 'This is Tom Murray speaking, I would like to speak with Dr Martin.' There was a decided change in tone, 'I'm very sorry but Dr Martin is not here at this time.' 'When you do expect him.' There was hesitation. 'I'm the housekeeper, I don't know what the doctor's schedule is. I'm sorry I can't be of any further help.'

He was staring vacantly at the slanted board. 'You in there Tom?' Jerry's voice cut across his thoughts and he saw the hand wave in front of his eyes. 'Don't think those doodles add up to the gable end of that building you're working on.' 'Sorry Jerry, I'm not quite with it today, as a matter of fact I think I'll cash in one of those holidays I'm due if that's alright with you. There's no deadline on the stuff I'm working on at the moment.'

It was mid-day. Tom bought the roses and drove to St Margarets. As he approached reception he found a young man dealing with enquiries. 'I've come to see Joanne Martin, what is her room number, please.' He ran his finger down the listing on a spread sheet and turned to files lying on the desk. 'Martin, J, yes I thought I had seen that name, she was discharged this morning' he said brightly. 'Look I'm her brother, I only got the message last night and have been driving north for the past eight hours. I didn't have a chance to speak to my father, but obviously the accident wasn't as bad as I was told.' 'Don't know about any accident, there's no notation here, just the routine D & C after the miscarriage.' Tom felt he could hardly breathe, his hands shook. 'You've left the flowers Mr Martin,' the young man called out as Tom left the building, but Tom only heard the word miscarriage, repeating over and over again in his head.

Tom phoned several times a day over the next week. It was always the same answer, Joanne was still unwell, couldn't speak to anyone. While Frank Martin's tone was cold and abrupt, there was a trace of sympathy in the housekeeper's voice when she answered. After ten days he received what looked like a hastily scribbled note from Joanne. She had persuaded the housekeeper to mail it for her. *"Bench, Tuesday 4 pm, Joanne"*

Tom was there at 3 o'clock. He paced up and down, craning his neck to look along the path in an effort to watch the gate and see anyone entering the park. 4 o'clock passed. He was checking his watch every five seconds, minutes seemed like hours, he was becoming more and more exasperated. 4:20 and Joanne came down the path. Tom ran to her gathering her in his arms, breathing in the remembered fragrance, kissing her eyes, ears, neck. At last he released her and was shocked to see how pale and thin she had become. She was nervous, continually twisting a handkerchief in her hands. 'Joanne, darling, why are we sitting here, let's go to my place where we can talk.' 'No' she said quickly, 'I'm sorry Tom, it's better we speak here, I can't stay away from the house too long. Father has been home day and night, I couldn't even use the phone to call you. He had to go out today but will be back very soon.' He held her hands, kissed her forehead. 'I'm sorry about the miscarriage, Joanne. The worst thing was not being able to be with you. I should have been there.' Tears welled up in her eyes, lips trembled, She knew she couldn't tell him. Momentarily she relived that evening, telling her father she was pregnant and wanted to marry Tom. She had expected him to show anger, make accusations, throw things. She wasn't prepared for the uncharacteristic Jovial behaviour. It was as if he hadn't heard her. He spoke of how exciting it was going to be in South Africa, talked of the excellent art college where she would continue her studies. He poured copious glasses of wine and offered port after dinner. He never once made any reference to the pregnancy or what she had said about marrying Tom. She was completely bewildered, didn't know what to think. Then later that evening she had felt faint, dizzy, nauseous. Frank had given her a shot which he said would calm things down. Her next recollection was of wakening in a strange bed surrounded by curtains. She could see the shadow of two women on the curtains, "that was a real bit of a botch up before and after that op. Can't see much chance of future babies for that little lady" one said to the other. Joanne shivered, how could she tell Tom, the man who wanted at least six children, the children she would never be able to give him.

Joanne sagged, she was drained of all strength and emotion, her voice flat. 'I can't fight my father any more, Tom. I've decided I will go with him to South Africa.' 'Nonsense,' he almost shouted, 'you leave that house now, today, I'll . . .' She stopped his protest by placing a hand on his lips. 'It's hopeless Tom. What happiness could we have in the future if we just run away. My father would find a way to drive a wedge between us somehow, it would ruin any feeling we had for each other.' Looking at the hurt expression on his face, the tight pain across her breast was unbearable, she wanted nothing more than to be in his arms, feel his strength, be shielded by his love. Tom bent over, elbows on knees, hands clasped, looking at the ground. 'I died a thousand deaths this past few weeks, Joanne. I was out of my mind when I heard you had lost the baby, I wanted to be there, to hold you, tell you there would be others, wanted you to know I would always be there for you.' Joanne sat rigid, calling on every ounce of strength not to cry, not to throw herself into his arms. 'Now It all sounds pretty futile. You seem to have made up your mind without considering my feelings, my love for you. Maybe it just wasn't enough for you, Joanne,' he said with a trace of bitterness. Joanne stood up quickly, she knew if she listened any more her resolve would weaken. 'I must get back to the house Tom, father will be home soon.' As she turned to leave in almost a whisper she said 'We leave for South Africa on Sunday, the noon plane. I'll write to you Tom.' Tom sat staring at the ground, his whole world crumbling. 'You sure the dear doctor will allow you to have a such an unsuitable pen-friend.' Joanne ran from the park blinded by tears.

The next few days and nights were a blur. Tom went to work but was not fully conscious of what he was doing. At night he ate very little, drank a lot in an effort to find sleep to blot out the anguish. He tried hard to resist but knew he had to see Joanne just one more time. On Saturday morning he phoned, his spirits sank as Frank Martin answered. 'I would like to speak to Joanne Dr Martin.' There was only the slightest pause, 'Just a minute, I'll call her.' Tom could hardly believe his ears, then his heart leapt at the sound of her voice. 'Hello Tom, how are you?' 'As well as can be expected, as the doctor might say,' his laugh sounded hollow. 'I was wondering if perhaps we could have a farewell drink tonight.' He couldn't see the trembling hand, her eyes tightly closed trying desperately to keep control. 'I can't come out tonight, Tom, father has arranged a dinner party for some friends and I must be here.' 'Right, well I understand. Would it be alright if I come to the airport tomorrow to say goodbye? I could see you in the departure lounge around 11 o'clock.' 'Yes, yes I'd like that,' was all she could say before hanging up the phone so that the sound of sobbing could not be heard.

It was almost midnight, Tom had fallen asleep on the couch and was awakened by the door bell being rung several times. He invited the two policemen in and closed the door. 'I wonder if you would be prepared to come with us to the General Infirmary. There has been a traffic accident involving an elderly man. We found no means of identification but your name and address were on a piece of paper in his pocket. Perhaps you will be able to identify him for us. The doctors believe his condition is serious and we would like to get in touch with his family.'

Tom dressed quickly and was driven to the Accident and Emergency section of the hospital. A nurse directed Tom and the policemen to a cubicle and pulled the screens. Tom looked at the deeply unconscious man. His face had been cleaned but there were various skin abrasions and bruising. 'It's my father, Billy Murray.'

One of the policemen made a notation in his notebook. 'Maybe we could have a word with you outside Mr Murray and we can explain what has been reported so far.' They walked to the end of the corridor and sat down on a bench. 'Would you like a cup of tea Mr Murray?' Tom shook his head. 'Witnesses at the scene reported that your father was staggering on the pavement, apparently in a drunken state, the doctors of course will determine the amount of alcohol in his bloodstream. Anyway, they said your father veered very quickly from the side of the building, walked off the kerb into the path of the bus. The driver, who is being treated for shock, says there was no way he could avoid hitting your father, in fact it was more a case of your father falling against the bumper and being thrown back towards the pavement. The witnesses at the scene tend to confirm that this is what happened.'

Tom merely nodded, and returned to the curtained cubicle. The young doctor was saying, 'Your father is seriously ill, Mr Murray. I know the police have given you their report and I can confirm he had recently consumed a large amount of alcohol. He has several broken ribs, the blow to the back of the head has caused extensive damage. We are awaiting the results of the X-Rays and a report from the Neurosurgeon. I'm afraid his chances are pretty slim' he said apologetically. The hours ticked by as Tom sat at Billy's side. He may have nodded off, he couldn't remember. He was thinking back to his childhood and of course thoughts of his mother. Billy died without regaining consciousness.

Tom went to the cafeteria, sipped his cup of tea staring at the wall, watching as the sunlight glinted on the wing of the aeroplane in the picture. He started forward suddenly, looking at his watch, it was 10 o'clock. He was to be at the airport at 11 o'clock to see Joanne. He dashed out of the hospital and hailed a taxi. 'Airport, quick as you can please.' Every traffic light seemed to be against them, the slow

It Was Meant To Be

Sunday drivers were out in force and refused to let anyone overtake. He looked at his watch again, 10:55, he ran into the terminal and dashed upstairs to the departure lounge looking only for Joanne. The lounge was almost deserted, there was no sign of her. He ran to the information desk. 'Look I was to meet someone here at 11 o'clock they're leaving on the noon flight to South Africa.' The girl looked at him somewhat disinterestedly. 'You've left it too late.' 'What do you mean too late it's only five past eleven now.'

It was a smirk rather than a smile, 'You forgot, the clocks went forward one hour at 2 o'clock this morning, summer time. It's now five past twelve. The South Africa flight left on time.'

Tom turned and walked very slowly from the airport terminal. He should have remembered the time change but he couldn't help thinking that even in death Billy had succeeded in robbing him of the precious time he needed.

Again only the distant cousins attended the funeral. It didn't take Tom long to clear out Billy's flat, what was there was hardly worth giving to the charity shop. He did find a christmas card box with some photographs wrapped in pink tissue paper. They were of himself with Alice and Billy at the seaside, himself licking an ice cream cone, others with the three of them smiling, apparently enJoying themselves. He had no recollection of those times, but he gently re-wrapped the pictures in the tissue paper and put them in his inside jacket pocket.

Chapter 11

Two months passed and he heard nothing from Joanne. He started to write several letters believing the post office would have a forwarding address for a period of time. He never mailed any of them, he decided Joanne should be the first to write, she was the one who had left.

Tom went for drinks with Jim and the others, dated other girls but there was an emptiness inside him and he withdrew more and more into himself. She was in his dreams, he woke in the morning with her name on his lips. Everywhere he looked there were reminders of Joanne, he was desperately unhappy. When six months had elapsed and he had not received a letter or even a postcard from Joanne, Tom decided he had to make a radical change in his life. He told no one of his plans, he wanted no link with the past, he wanted to make a completely fresh start in every sense of the word, it was like being reborn.

Compiling the necessary data was a formality and within a comparatively short time he was granted permission to emigrate to Canada. Upon arrival at Malton Airport after clearing customs and immigration Tom caught a taxi to the YMCA. He was feeling the effects of jet lag and slept for the next twelve hours. The next day, as he had been instructed to do, Tom headed for the immigration office. He had been advised they assisted new immigrants with a listing of possible accommodation, if required, and also where they might seek employment. This was Tom's first priority and within days he had been offered a position with the prestigious firm of Dunbar & Son, Architects. Having his first month's salary credited to his account he moved from the YMCA to an apartment on Wellesley Street, close enough to the underground which would take him to work. He did not feel confident enough just yet to buy a car and start driving on the wrong side of the road.

It was all so new and somewhat exciting. Toronto was a very cosmopolitan city, a complete hodgepodge of every ethnic group. While fully integrated, many of the various groups zealously worked at maintaining a national identity. There were Italian clubs, German clubs, Polish, Irish and Scottish and many others. Tom couldn't grasp the meaning of native born Canadians describing themselves as half of one nationality and half of another, even in some cases identifying themselves with four different ethnic groups. The same applied to restaurants, every conceivable desire for European, Far East and Indian cuisine could be satisfied.

It was exciting. A vast number of young men and women in the same position as Tom, all trying to find their way in the new world, bonds of friendship were easily formed. Tom was keen to join his new friends in soaking up the atmosphere of this multi-racial city and inevitably he attended the Scottish club where, as a new arrival from the 'old country', he was warmly welcomed. As in the other clubs he had visited, some of those who claimed to be of a particular nationality had never actually been to these countries but they knew the folk songs and danced the traditional country dances. While on the one hand they were fervently Canadian it seemed there was a fierce determination to maintain this tangible link with the world of their ancestors.

There were times when Tom would be reminded of Joanne, a girl laughing in a certain way, a certain hair colouring, sometimes the whiff of a particular perfume. He recognised it as part of a past life, impossible to completely forget, but stored reverently, deep in his sub-conscious memory.

It was a warm September evening, Tom and Al Montini walked down Bloor Street and sat at a sidewalk cafe for a beer. 'I'm building a cabin up at Thousand Islands,' Al said, 'I've got some mates coming to help me with this long holiday weekend, fancy coming?'

'Thousand Islands, where's that' said Tom. It's north of here, located in the narrow stretch of Lake Ontario close to the St Lawrence river. Gorgeous spot at this time of the year. We'll be sleeping rough, but lots of beer and barbecues, you'll enjoy it.' 'Sounds great, tell me what to bring. I'll shop on the way home on Friday.' 'Best do it Thursday, we'll be leaving direct from the site on Friday, get the good of the weekend.'

This was new territory for Tom and as they drove north he was bemused to see place names like Agincourt, Northumberland, Brighton, Portsmouth, he began to wonder if he was still in Canada. Al had explained that the foundation of the cabin had been poured and the walls partially erected during the summer, the roof trusses had been delivered so hopefully they could complete that section this weekend, it wasn't such a large cabin. They were towing a trailer with wood, tools and a few crates of beer. Bob and Charlie were in the following car with a similar trailer behind them. It was dark by the time they arrived and Tom was surprised when Al told him to start unloading the trailer into a little putt-putt boat tied to a dock. 'We'll be going to that island,' and he pointed to a shape just visible in the light from a shrouded moon.

Al stayed on the island after the first trip to prepare the barbecue and put the beer in the coolers packed with ice they had bought at the last gas station. It took eight trips to transport everything from the trailers and by then they were thankful to flop down on the soft earth and drink the ice cold beer. The coals were burning hot, the ears of corn, wrapped in foil, were cooking nicely. Al slapped the four T-bone steaks on the grill and spirals of blue smoke rose from the fat dripping onto the coals. The mouthwatering smell made them all suddenly realise how hungry they were. Talk tailed off, each of them lost in their own thoughts as they sat looking at the reflection of the now cloudless moon on the water. 'Don't know about you lot but I'm hitting the sack,' said Al, 'got to get that roof up tomorrow.' The sleeping bags were arranged around the fire and soon the only sounds were the call of the bull frogs, the crickets and a few snores.

They worked well as a team and by the end of the weekend the roof trusses were up, the panel boards had been nailed. There had been time in between for the occasional swim to cool off and boat trips between the different islands. There were numerous calls from other 'week-enders' to share barbecues, 'bring your own weiners and beer' being the usual cry.

Tom was sorry when it came time to pack up, he had enjoyed the uncomplicated, natural lifestyle but he thought of the old cliche, "all good things must come to an end". 'Got yourself a girlfriend yet?' Al asked as they drove back to Toronto. 'Not as yet. The guys at the site keep trying to double date me with their girlfriends' sisters, but I'm in no rush.' There was a fleeting image of Joanne in his mind's eye but he was not going to think about that any more. 'Bet you haven't been to the Italian club yet, some gorgeous looking gals there. Come with me on Thursday night, I guarantee you'll find somebody you like.' Tom laughed, 'I'm game but no blind dates, ok?' They were sitting at the bar, Al was speaking in Italian to an extremely attractive girl with an olive complexion, dark eyes and very long black wavy hair. She was listening to Al but her eyes were on Tom. 'She's only been in the country a few weeks and is a bit shy, thinks her English is not yet good enough,' Al said to Tom then turned and asked the girl to dance. Tom's eyes swept the room and stopped, she was at a table with two other girls but looking

It Was Meant To Be

directly at him. The straight blond hair and pale skin set her apart from the others. Tom approached and asked her to dance. He was pleased to find she was quite tall. 'You don't look Italian,' Tom started, 'but I know northern Italians are fairer than those from the south,' he added quickly. 'You neither look nor sound Italian yourself and I'm Canadian,' she said. Tom smiled, you're right, I'm Scottish. You're the first person I've met who's called herself "Canadian", mostly I find people go back as far as grandparents in claiming a particular nationality.' 'Yes, that's the norm around here, and if you look at it that way I am a mixture of Scots and English, but I think it is about time people born here identify with being Canadian.' The music stopped. 'Can I buy you a drink?' Tom asked. He waved to Al as he and the girl sat down at a table near the end of the bar. Al winked and gave a thumbs up sign. 'When did you arrive in the country and what do you do?' she asked in a forthright, confident manner. 'Been here just over fifteen months now. I work with the architectural firm, Dunbar. Funny thing about names he smiled, my mother's maiden name was Dunbar. By the way the name's Tom Murray,' and he held out his hand. 'I'm Sarah,' slight hesitation, 'Sarah Harper,' she smiled shaking his hand. 'I know some people who used to work at Dunbars. Pretty big outfit, on University Avenue isn't it?' 'Yeah, they have the top three floors of the Milton building. Fantastic views over the city from the top floor, not that I'm in such an elevated position, but things have been going well recently so I've got high hopes of reaching the top floor one of these days. Right now I share an office with Al,' and he indicated his friend at the bar. 'Is it true that old Dunbar the Chairman still runs the company himself, ever met him?' 'I was introduced to Mr Dunbar once. He's well liked around the place and seems a decent sort, but other than that I don't know much about him. I've never met his son.'

'His son, what do you mean?' Sarah asked. 'Well, it's Dunbar and Son so I assume he has a son somewhere.' There was an easy familiarity between them as they danced and talked for the rest of the evening until finally Sarah said, 'Thanks for the drinks, Tom, I think it is time I rejoined my friends they look as though they are ready to leave.' 'How about having dinner with me sometime, or maybe go to a movie?' 'Yes, I'd like that, in fact there's a new film at the Palace I'd like to see, that's if you haven't seen it.' 'Couldn't tell you when I last saw a movie so it's unlikely I've seen it. How about Thursday. I haven't got a car yet, would it be alright if we meet there?' 'Yes, great, I'll see you at the Palace, 7 o'clock.'

'That's a good looking guy, Sarah, and quite a dancer. I notice you weren't keen to bring him over and introduce him to your friends,' Angela laughed. 'Too true, I'm keeping him all to myself. Guess what, he works at Dunbars.'

There was the background sound of a string orchestra, the lights were dimmed and the glow of the burning logs cast a shadow on the wall, the thick drapes were drawn shutting out the falling snow. Tom set the tray with coffee and brandy on the floor as he Joined Sarah in front of the fire. 'I can't believe it's almost Christmas. These past months have just flown by, thanks to you,' he said kissing the top of her head. Sarah looked at him, a small smile playing around her lips as she turned onto her knees straddling his body. She kissed his eyes as she unbuttoned his shirt, her tongue traced the outline of his ear, her hands travelled down inside his thighs. There was a gasp as he took her in his arms kissing her softly at first at then with a deep passion. Slowly they undressed each other, caressing each part of the other's body as it was revealed, each of them flirting with erotic, rhythmic movements until with both bodies arched in anticipation, he entered her and the mutual climax shuddered through them. Sarah had fallen asleep in his arms. Tom closed his eyes and as in a dream relived the hightened moments of their love making. In shock he suddenly realised he was visualising Joanne. He eased his arm from under Sarah's head, got up and put more logs on the fire. Pouring himself a brandy he sat in the chair staring into flames. He had not thought about Joanne almost from the time he had met Sarah. Why now, why should he be reminded of what he had lost, the pain of that loss was obviously nearer the surface than he had admitted to himself. He looked at the sleeping form, the silken blond hair glinting in the firelight. Maybe nothing would ever be the same as your first love, that would always have a special corner of your heart, but Tom knew that world could never be regained, he knew he had a different kind of love for Sarah and she was with him now. They showered together and dressed. Tom made fresh coffee while Sarah stood looking out of the window. 'Thank goodness the snow has stopped, doesn't look too deep either so I'll get home alright.' He wrapped his arms around her, kissing the back of her neck. 'You could spend the rest of the night here, I don't like the thought of you driving in that sort of weather.' 'Hey, I'm the Canadian remember, I'm used to this sort of thing,' she laughed and picked up the cup of coffee. 'Come sit here,' she patted the cushion beside her on the couch. They were silent for a while and she noted an unusually serious expression on Tom's face. 'Sarah, I've never put it into words before, but if you haven't realised it by now, I want to say I love you. I love you very, very much.' She sat quietly looking at the burning logs. 'We've never spoken much about your family, you told me your mother died when you were quite young and you've only briefly talked about your father, but you've never asked me to meet him. Maybe I'm presuming too much.' Sarah was quiet for several seconds and Tom started to take his arm from around her shoulders. She caught his hand and looked up, a hint of tears in her eyes. 'Before I say anything else Tom, I want you to know I've been waiting a long time to hear you say you love me. I'm not embarrassed to say I've used every wile known to woman to make you fall in love with me, I was beginning to run out of ideas' and she laughed. 'I've never loved anyone as I love you, Tom' As he started to draw her into his arms she jumped up and sat in the chair facing him. 'Tom before we go any further there are a few things I have to tell you.' He sat quietly, looking at her. 'First off, my name is not Harper. Remember the first night we met you told me you worked at Dunbars and your mother's maiden name was Dunbar. Well that gave me the idea to use the name Harper, it was my Mother's maiden name. You see Tom, my name is Dunbar, David Dunbar is my father.' Tom stared at her. 'Normally I would have come right out and told you who my father was, but I didn't know how you would react considering you were working at the office. I knew right away I wanted to get to know you better and I didn't want to scare you off. I'm sorry, Tom, it was probably a stupid thing to do and it's been so difficult keeping up the pretense. But that's all different now. I can't wait for you to come home and meet my father. He already knows I've been seeing a lot of you and wonders why I haven't brought you home.' Tom sat silently, trying to get some order into the different thoughts that were racing through his brain. 'There are some things I don't understand. You share an apartment with Angela, why don't you live with your father?' 'Dad lives in a stuffy old house over in Rosewood, he's always encouraged me to be independent and never objected to my moving out and living my own life.' 'You say your father knows about me and he hasn't objected to our being together?' 'Why should he. From what I hear you are held in very high regard and have the reputation of being a very good architect, even if you were the first one to tell me so,' she laughed. 'As for my father, my happiness is all that matters to him.' After several minutes when they each sat engrossed in their own thoughts, Sarah said, 'What's going through your head, Tom?' 'You're right about one thing Sarah, I would probably have run a country mile if you had told me that first night that you were the boss's daughter. I'm not altogether certain that I shouldn't still do that.' 'Too late for that Mr Murray,' she said sitting on his knee with her arms around his neck, 'from the minute you said you loved me you were trapped. I've waited so long for those words, you don't know how I felt like screaming every time you packed me off home without a word. I was certain, I just knew I was going to fall in love with you the first moment our eyes met in the Italian club' and she kissed him.

Chapter 12

Tom had nothing to worry about. David Dunbar had a high regard for Tom and been impressed with his skills and the contribution he made to the success of the company. He was more than delighted to hear of Sarah and Tom's love for each other. To everyones delight it was a short engagement and on their marriage David Dunbar offered Tom a position on the Board of the Company. David asked Tom if he would consider using the name of Dunbar so that the firm would finally be Dunbar and Son. Tom immediately agreed to change from Murray to Dunbar explaining it was an easy decision since Dunbar had been his mother's maiden name.

Young Davey (David) had been named for his grandfather. At 10 years old he was excitedly running around the kitchen. We must go soon mom, have you found my lucky hockey stick, I've got to have that to score tonight. Where's dad he said he would be at the game tonight. Ok, Ok, Davey just settle down, we've got loads of time.

David Dunbar slapped Tom on the shoulder, that's one fine contract you secured Tom sure glad you're on my team. How about we go for a celebratory drink son. Tom smiled thanks Mr Dunar but I've got to rush off. Young Davey's playing in a big hockey match tonight and I promised him and Sarah I'd get there in good time. Well, right then, I'll come with you, his proud grandpa should be there too, hope he scores.

The phone rang, Sarah I'm sorry darling, there's a big deal going on at the office. Dad and I can't leave at the moment. Please explain to Davey and I promise we will be there for the 'face off'. Tell him I know he is good for two goals. Sarah hung up, right, Davey, lets get going before that snow starts. Dad and grandpa will meet us at the stadium.

Tom and David drove the 25 miles to the stadium. It was snowing heavily and when they arrived the carpark was full and what looked like security cars at the front entrance. A group of security officers stopped Tom from entering "there's been an accident inside sir, no one is allowed in." Tom shouted at them, my wife and son are in there I want to get to them. I'm sorry sir, part of the roof has collapsed under the snow, the maintenance men are working to secure the site. There are injuries and emergency medical staff are in attendance. No one is allowed in, you can park in that enclosure, we'll get word to you as soon as possible.

Tom and David joined others at the catering cafe outside of the grounds to await news. An hour passed and a policeman came to advise that the area had been secured and they could come to pick up their children and family members.

There was much tension inside the building. Women in tears, men calling out names and screams of joy from those finding loved ones and cries of despair in discovering soneone was injured. Tom turned around, Mr Dun—Dad, maybe you should wait by the car and I'll bring Sarah and Davey as soon as I find them. Ok Tom, make it quick please. David turned around and picked his way slowly towards the outside door. A policeman was standing with a number of the young players around him. David started towards where the car was parked but the crowd swell propelled him to the door. He was going down the path towards the car when there was a loud shout of "Grandpa wait for me" and young Davey bounced into his outstretched arms. Where's Mom, Where's Dad are they in the car. Calm down Davey, here let's get into the car and wait. While they sat Davey told his Grandpa 'we were just about to face off on the ice when there was a loud bang and part of the roof fell on the people sitting on the bleechers. It weren't where Mom was sitting, I know cause she waved to me when we came out to the ice and she was moving to the other side'. Ok Davey I'm sure everything's fine. Mom and Dad will be here soon. Now I want you to stay in the car and I'll go up to the cafeteria and get us something to eat and drink, what would you like Davey. Well I'm not too hungry, a cheeseburger, fries and a coke would be enough for me.

Davey was curled up asleep on the back seat. David had the radio on listening to the broadcaster describe the scene at the Ice Stadium and his report said three people had been killed and several had serious injuries. He turned off the radio and sat staring at people getting into cars and driving off. He was tired and about to nod off when he caught sight of Tom walking slowly to the car. Davey woke up as Tom got into the car. Dad, Dad did you see it, I scored a goal, we won the game. Where were you, I was looking for you. I'm sorry Davey, Grandpa and I had to work late at the office. Ok ok, Davey shouted, where's Mom, she saw me, she'll tell you, where is she. Be quiet Davey, give your Dad a chance to speak. There was stress and a break in Davids voice that he could not conceal. Tom put his arm around Davey's shoulders and held him close while looking at David. Moms had an accident Davey, she's gone to the hospital and we're going there now to see her. You lie down on the back seat and have a nap, I'll wake you when we get to the hospital. Davey was asleep almost at once. I'll drive Dad. I saw Sarah just briefly as she was going into the ambulance. She was unconscious and the medic told me it looked like head and back injuries but wouldn't or couldn't say more. We'll find out more at the hospital.

Tom was walking very slowly to the car. David looked at his face and stifled a cry. As Davey jumped from the car Tom wrapped his arms around him hugging him tightly, He looked at David and shook his head, I'm sorry Davey, Mom was crushed by falling debris, she has died.

Tom, David and Davey were just finishing dinner. David raised his glass. "well great having you aboard Young Davey. You're 18 now, graduating shortly and a new David Dunbar, fully qualified Architect will be joining Dunbar and Son, maybe a new letterhead should show "Dunbar and Sons", they all drank to that. I agree, said Tom, but I hear you want to take time for a bit of travelling Davey, and he has earned some time off Dad. Yes I've been talking with some of the guys and we would like to do the old country, Europe, New Zealand and Australia then back here to work. Guess about a year should do it. Well yes, David said, I think you deserve that young fella and we'll hold your place 'til you return.

The 14 months went quickly, Davey thoroughly enjoyed travelling through all the countries but was happy to return to Toronto and start serious work at Dunbars. 'Dad I'm thinking of getting an apartment in town. Would be easier getting to work and there is so much more social goings on in town'. You're right Davey, not much fun staying with me alone in this old house. You go, it's time for you to enjoy life, meet some nice girls, eh? Can't wait to meet that special one.

Chapter 13

Tom heard himself saying—that special one, he sat up, looked around. The dreams were so real, so vivid he wasn't quite sure where he was.

Dad you're alright. Davey had his hands on Toms shoulders and held him flat on the bed. Tom rolled his head from side to side, opened his eyes and looked at Davey. 'What's going on, what happened', 'Dad, its alright, you had a fall and hit your head but Doc says no broken bones and you'll be OK' 'When did this happen Davey, I feel I've been away for years'. 'You've been unconscious for about four hours Dad. You must have had some wild dreams the way you rolled about, shouting names'. 'Yes, yes Davey, your right, I need something to drink'. 'Non alcoholic Dad, Doc says you shouldn't drink when you are taking the pills he's left for you'. 'Tonic water would be fine Davey. I was sure dreaming something big, it felt like I had lived my whole life again, Funny, one thing I can't figure out, I kept hearing a womans voice it was like somebody I knew years ago'. 'That would be Heather's voice you heard Dad, she was here with me and Doc said we should talk naturally until you came round. She's upstairs right now Dad. Considering how late it was I suggested she should stay here in the guest wing, I knew it would be alright with you. Dad it's getting late and probably not a good time to go into a lot of detailed explanations. When we've all had a good nights sleep we can sit quietly and clear everything up'. 'You're right Davey, let's sleep on it and tackle things tomorrow'.

Tom came into the kitchen 'something smells good'. 'I've got bacon egg and toast for you Dad and some strong tea.' 'Good on you Davey, I'm ready for that. Sure was a bumper of a sleep I had. Well, now that I'm at ground level you can introduce me again to your special girl, you said she's called Heather, did I get that right. I must have made a fne impression on her last night. Which part of Toronto is she living in' No, Dad, Heather lives with her Mother in Hamilton. She came through on the train to meet you and I was going to drive her home. She called her Mother to let her know she would be staying over and her Mother says she will drive over today, meet us and take Heather home. Just as well it's the weekend and no work to worry about'. 'Great, son, now tell me a bit about Heather, she didn't sound Canadian'. 'No Dad, she comes from Australia. She came to Canada on one of those 'exchange student' deals at McMaster University in Hamilton. She liked it over here so much, maybe I had something to do with that—well anyway she convinced her Mother that she should stay and her Mother decided to Join her. She is a widow, Heather told me her Dad was killed in a car crash when she was 8 years old'.

There was a knock at the door, it opened and Heather came in. 'I heard voices and thought you must be awake Mr Dunbar. How are you feeling? Tom looked at her for a long moment, 'I'm fine Heather, sorry for that nonsense falling off the ladder and I can assure you I was sober'. They all laughed. 'I'm glad you stayed here last night and look forward to meeting your Mother. Those pills the Doc left made sure I had a good nights sleep and after a hearty breakfast I feel almost normal. How about you two' " Davey and Heather both spoke at once, fine, just fine. Great to see you looking so well Dad, you gave us quite a scare'. 'Ok, Tom said that's all past now let's head for a comfortable seat in the living room and I think you should re-introduce me to Heather.'.

'Dad I did mention to you more than once that I was dating someone I liked very much'. 'Not for the first time, Tom interupted'. 'Well anyway Dad, this is Heather and she lives with her Mother in Hamilton. We met some time back when she came through to Toronto to visit mutual friends and its gone on from there, and we're hoping it will go on for the rest of our lives'. Tom's hand shot in the air, 'hold on there slow down a bit, this is going on faster than I can think'. The front door bell rang. Davey jumped up, 'I'll get it'. They came into the room, 'Dad this is Mrs Thornton, Heather's mother'. She came into the room, hesitated, stood very still, her face flushed and after a moments silence, she took one step forward and called out 'TOM'. Tom was half way out of the deep arm chair his eyes wide open he fell back into the chair shouting 'Joanne'. Davey ran to his Dad, Heather hurried over to her mother hugging her tightly. "What's going on here Dad, do you two know each other'. 'Mum, it can't be possible can it?' Heather took her arm, 'Mum sit down please what's this all about for goodness sake'. The four of them sat in silence for a few moments. 'Joanne started, you are the Tom Murray I knew a long time ago aren't you'. Tom had some difficulty in speaking, 'yes I'm that guy and you're Joanne Martin right?' Davey jumped up, 'Dad, you're Tom Dunbar not Tom Murray and this is Mrs Thornton not Joanne Martin. You're both mixed up, let's start all over again and clear up this mess'.

It Was Meant To Be

Tom stood up walked over and sat beside Joanne. 'I think we will both agree that you two kids have the right to know the whole story and it's going to take a very long time, even Joanne and I have to fill in some of the blanks'. Tom looked around 'I would like to suggest Joanne that you Heather stay here tonight in the guest wing and return to Hamilton tomorrow, how does that sound?' 'Well I don't have to rush back tonight, what do you think Heather'. 'I like the idea Mum, it will be good for all of us to have this time together'. 'Davey you know I have a table booked at the Sheraton on Saturday nights. Why don't you take Heather into town to the Sheraton and have dinner. Joanne and I can have a quiet drink, eat here and have some time to talk over old times'. 'Dad you've nothing here to cook for dinner except that frozen fish and chips package that you keep for what you call 'specials'. Joanne smiled, 'I think fish and chips would suit us just fine Davey'. 'Ok Dad we'll go now and be back around ten.

'Joanne, maybe I should start OK'. She smiled and nodded. 'I jiust wish you could have shared the dream I had a couple of hours ago while I was unconscious. I seemed to relive my whole life up until the moment you walked into this room Joanne'. Tom went over the main parts of his life just as he had seen them in his dream. There was silence when he finished.

Joanne wiped a tear from her eye, 'now I guess it's my turn. I can see everything Tom, right up to our last meeting in the park and then I was virtually hauled away to South Africa. Believe me Tom I wouldn't have gone except I thought, because of a conversation I overheard in the hospital, that I would not be able to give you the children we both wanted. I was devastated. In South Africa I couldn't write at first Tom, my Dad shadowed me every waking minute he didn't want me to keep in touch with anyone at home. This went on for some six months then I managed to send a note to Mrs Main the Librarian you mentioned. She had retired by then but they passed on my message and she wrote to say that you had left suddenly without telling anyone where you were going. I wanted so much to hear from you but there was nothing else I could do. When I had finished college in South Africa I worked with a group of architects, I enjoyed the work. There was little social life and, well, I didn't want to meet or be involved with anyone I wanted to be with you. Then my Dad arranged for me to meet Derek Thornton, a junior doctor in his practice. Arranged is the right term in that he intended I should marry Derek which, after quiite a long time, I did. We lived with my father and Derek became a full partner in the practice. I continued with my work. Then the unexpected happened, I couldn't believe it but I was pregnant. Heather was born and we both loved her very much. Later Dad had a serious illness and died within two years. At that time there was some political unrest in the country and Derek decided we should move to Australia for Heather and our own safety. He was a very kind and considerate man and a good father to Heather. We had been married eight years when, unfortunately, he was killed in a car crash accident. When Heather was at University an exchange student programme came about. She was anxious to see another part of the world and as I had always had a yearning to see Canada myself I agreed that she should go and I would travel over at some point to visit her. Every time she wrote or we spoke on the phone Heather was telling me how she had met 'wonderful' Davey and how they enyoyed being together. Then suddenly it was "we're planning a future together". so here I am.

Tom and Joanne were sitting close together on the sofa. He held her hand, It's so difficult to understand Tom how at times life can be so cruel and then it all changes so unexpectedly. When I think how all those years ago we loved each other so much but were forced to part, but now we can bury the past, can't we?. Davey and Heather obviously love each other very much and I think we're both glad about that. 'You're so very right, Joanne it's the best thing that could have happened. I know Davey and Heather are right for each other'. Joanne sighed, there was a tear in her eye. It could have been us Tom, but now our daughter and son will be one and their children will be our very own much loved grandchildren. Tom leaned over, his lips brushed her ear as he whispered, Yes, my dear Joanne, it was meant to be.

The End